Rural Crime and Poverty
Violence, Drugs, and Other Issues

Youth in Rural North America

Title List

Getting Ready for the Fair: Crafts, Projects, and Prize-Winning Animals

Growing Up on a Farm: Responsibilities and Issues

Migrant Youth: Falling Between the Cracks

Rural Crime and Poverty: Violence, Drugs, and Other Issues

Rural Teens and Animal Raising: Large and Small Pets

Rural Teens and Nature: Conservation and Wildlife Rehabilitation

Rural Teens on the Move:
Cars, Motorcycles, and Off-Road Vehicles

Teen Life Among the Amish and Other Alternative Communities:
Choosing a Lifestyle

Teen Life on Reservations and in First Nation Communities:
Growing Up Native

Teen Minorities in Rural North America: Growing Up Different

Teens and Rural Education: Opportunities and Challenges

Teens and Rural Sports: Rodeos, Horses, Hunting, and Fishing

Teens Who Make a Difference in Rural Communities:
Youth Outreach Organizations and Community Action

Rural Crime and Poverty
Violence, Drugs, and Other Issues

by Jean Otto Ford

Mason Crest Publishers

Philadelphia

Mason Crest Publishers Inc.
370 Reed Road
Broomall, Pennsylvania 19008
(866) MCP-BOOK (toll free)
www.masoncrest.com

First printing
1 2 3 4 5 6 7 8 9 10
ISBN 978-1-4222-0011-7 (series)

Library of Congress Cataloging-in-Publication Data

Ford, Jean (Jean Otto)
  Rural crime and poverty : violence, drugs, and other issues / by Jean Otto Ford.
       p. cm. — (Youth in rural North America)
  Includes index.
  ISBN 978-1-4222-0016-2
  1. Rural youth—United States—Juvenile literature. 2. Poor youth—United States—Juvenile literature. 3. Rural youth—Drug use—United States—Juvenile literature. 4. Juvenile delinquency—United States—Juvenile literature. 5. Rural crimes—United States—Juvenile literature. I. Title. II. Series.
  HV1431.F67 2006
  364.360973'091734—dc22
                                        2005029002

Cover and interior design by MK Bassett-Harvey.
Produced by Harding House Publishing Service, Inc.
www.hardinghousepages.com

Cover image design by Peter Spires Culotta.
Cover photography by iStock Photography (Mark Jensen and Gary Unwin).
Printed in Malaysia by Phoenix Press.

Contents

Introduction **6**

1. Defining the Differences: Diversity Among Poor, Rural Youth **9**
2. Dealing Desperation: Drugs and Poverty and Rural Youth **27**
3. Deceptive Dangers: Marijuana, Alcohol, and Tobacco Use **49**
4. Doomed Daring: Rural Poverty and Nonviolent Crime **65**
5. Deadly Dysfunction: Rural Poverty and Violence **73**

Further Reading **86**

For More Information **87**

Glossary **88**

Bibliography **90**

Index **94**

Picture Credits **95**

Author & Consultant Biographies **96**

Introduction

by Celeste Carmichael

Results of a survey published by the Kellogg Foundation reveal that most people consider growing up in the country to be idyllic. And it's true that growing up in a rural environment does have real benefits. Research indicates that families in rural areas consistently have more traditional values, and communities are more closely knit. Rural youth spend more time than their urban counterparts in contact with agriculture and nature. Often youth are responsible for gardens and farm animals, and they benefit from both their sense of responsibility and their understanding of the natural world. Studies also indicate that rural youth are more engaged in their communities, working to improve society and local issues. And let us not forget the psychological and aesthetic benefits of living in a serene rural environment!

The advantages of rural living cannot be overlooked—but neither can the challenges. Statistics from around the country show that children in a rural environment face many of the same difficulties that are typically associated with children living in cities, and they fare worse than urban kids on several key indicators of positive youth development. For example, rural youth are more likely than their urban counterparts to use drugs and alcohol. Many of the problems facing rural youth are exacerbated by isolation, lack of jobs (for both parents and teens), and lack of support services for families in rural communities.

When most people hear the word "rural," they instantly think "farms." Actually, however, less than 12 percent of the population in rural areas make their livings through agriculture. Instead, service jobs are the top industry in rural North America. The lack of opportunities for higher paying jobs can trigger many problems: persistent poverty, lower educational standards, limited access to health care, inadequate housing, underemployment of teens, and lack of extracurricular possibilities. Additionally, the lack of—or in some cases surge of—diverse populations in rural communities presents its own set of challenges for youth and communities. All these concerns lead to the greatest threat to rural communities: the mass exodus of the post–high school population. Teens relocate for educational, recreational, and job opportunities, leaving their hometown indefinitely deficient in youth capital.

This series of books offers an in-depth examination of both the pleasures and challenges for rural youth. Understanding the realities is the first step to expanding the options for rural youth and increasing the likelihood of positive youth development.

CHAPTER 1
Defining the Differences: Diversity Among Poor, Rural Youth

It's hard when you live so far from everything. There's not much for kids to do. We don't even have stores around here. The mall? [Laughs.] That's an hour away; sh--, the closest McDonald's is thirty miles from here. Besides, who has any money anyway? And how would we get there? —Bridget, a rural New Mexico girl

A high school student can't read because her family can't afford the glasses she needs. Another can't drink his tap water because it's contaminated. An eighth-grader can't call his friends because his family has no phone. A tenth-grader can't get online because she doesn't have electricity, let alone a computer.

Childhood poverty is most prevalent in rural communities.

You might think these youths live in a developing country halfway across the world. They don't. They live right here, in rural America.

Rural Poverty in America

According to a recent Pennsylvania State University study presented to the American Sociological Association in Toronto, Canada, nearly 25 percent of U.S. children live in poverty, and over 1.2 million Canadian children are poor. Additionally, nearly 40 percent of all American kids will experience some degree of short-term poverty before they reach age sixteen.

Despite what most people think, childhood poverty is greater (percentage-wise) in rural America than in urban America. From the backwoods of **Appalachia** to the Mississippi River Delta, from American Indian reservations in the southwest to **Aboriginal** villages in western Canada, America's rural poor span the continent. And rural children are more likely than their urban counterparts to be poor.

According to the U.S. Census 2000, three out of five rural children live in poverty. (Here the term "children" refers to those who are younger than eighteen.) That's 60 percent of rural kids, or two-and-a-half million children in the United States alone. Of the nation's 250 poorest counties, 244 are rural.

Although these counties spread across the nation, most **demographers** agree that rural poverty in the United States tends to cluster in six regions: the **Deep South**, the Southwest, the border defined by the Rio Grande, California's central valley, the northern plain states, and central Appalachia. Many of Canada's rural poor live in Aboriginal settlements scattered across its provinces or in isolated, single-industry communities such as fishing or foresting villages. Chronic pockets of long-term poverty exist in all these areas, and their poverty rates can be two to three times higher than national averages.

The American poor have many faces; poverty doesn't care about race. Whether Euro-American, Latino, Mexican American, African American, Asian American, or Inuit, North American Indian, or other Aboriginal peoples, poverty claims many victims.

"Rural" communities can be found in many different regions.

Defining Rural

Many people misunderstand rural America and its residents. For example, one poll found the majority of U.S. residents think rural regions are agricultural, yet, according to the National Advisory Committee on Rural Social Services, only 6.3 percent of rural Americans live on farms. Others picture rural towns as idyllic, safe havens characterized by unlocked doors and pies cooling in open windows, but violent crime and substance-abuse rates are fast approaching—and in some cases passing—those of American cities.

Rural teens must deal with issues like alcohol abuse.

Popular assumptions of picture-postcard prosperity frequently downplay or deny the heartbreaking struggles of the hidden poor.

Stereotypes about what it means to be rural and poor are everywhere, and, like all stereotypes, they rarely depict what's real. Many differences among and within America's rural communities prevent generalization about the people and their environments. Even the term "rural" defies specific definition. America's remote regions are simply too diverse for one adjective.

Nonetheless, government agencies look to two main characteristics when officially determining if a region is rural. How far away an area is from other population centers is one measure. Low population density (the number of residents per square mile) is the other.

For example, the U.S. Census Bureau defines "rural" as any one area with a population density of less than 1,000 people per square mile that's also surrounded by census "blocks" with densities fewer than 500 people per square mile. The Office of Management and Budget defines its rural equal (termed "non-metropolitan") as counties "outside the boundaries of metropolitan areas and having no cities with as many as 50,000 residents." Whether using remoteness or density, both measures are relevant when classifying rural-ness.

According to the USDA Economic Research Association, "rural" U.S. regions span over 2,052 counties, contain 75 percent of all U.S. land, and house nearly 20 percent of the country's population. National Libraries and Archives Canada reports that one-third of Canadians live in rural and remote areas. Think of the differences in climate and geography across these two nations! Think of the varying natural resources and peoples!

For example, consider two communities: a desolate fishing village in Newfoundland and an impoverished mountain town of central Appalachia. How can they compare? Now examine a *shantytown* along the Rio Grande and a struggling farm community in the Midwest. Then consider the Aboriginal village in Manitoba or an American Indian reservation in South Dakota. These places might all technically be "rural," but that's where their similarity ends.

Table 1. U.S. Poverty Thresholds 2004

U.S. Poverty Thresholds for 2004 by Size of Family and Number of Related Children under 18 Years

Size of Family Unit	Related Children under Eighteen Years Old								
	None	One	Two	Three	Four	Five	Six	Seven	Eight +
One person									
Under 65 years	9,827								
65 years and over	9,060								
Two persons									
Householder under 65 years	12,649	13,020							
Householder 65 years and over	11,418	12,971							
Three persons	14,776	15,205	15,219						
Four persons	19,484	19,803	19,157	19,223					
Five persons	23,497	23,838	23,108	23,543	22,199				
Six persons	27,025	27,133	26,573	26,037	25,241	24,768			
Seven persons	31,096	31,290	30,621	30,154	29,285	28,271	27,159		
Eight persons	34,778	35,086	34,454	33,901	33,115	32,119	31,082	30,818	
Nine persons or more	41,836	42,039	41,480	41,010	40,240	39,179	38,220	37,983	36,520

Source: U.S. Census Bureau.

Neither geography nor people groups, neither occupation nor lifestyle can paint "rural" America with one sweeping brush. Poverty, on the other hand, is easier to define.

Defining Poverty

The U.S. Census Bureau uses measures called "poverty thresholds" to determine poverty status. These thresholds—or minimum income

This idyllic image of the countryside does not depict the challenges faced by real rural teens.

levels in dollars—vary with family size and ages of related family members, but they do not vary with geographical region. The same thresholds apply to all U.S. people regardless of locality; that includes rural residents.

If a family's total before-tax income is less than the established threshold for that family type, the government classifies the family as living in poverty. If total family income equals or exceeds its corresponding threshold, that family is technically not living in poverty. Any difference in dollars between the threshold and actual family income becomes an income deficit (if earnings are below poverty thresholds) or an income surplus (if earnings are above the threshold).

For example, family Z has five members: Dad, Mom, their two children (ages eleven and fourteen), and Mom's adult sister. Looking at Table 1, the size of the family unit is five, and the number of related children under age eighteen is two. This family's poverty threshold is therefore $23,108.

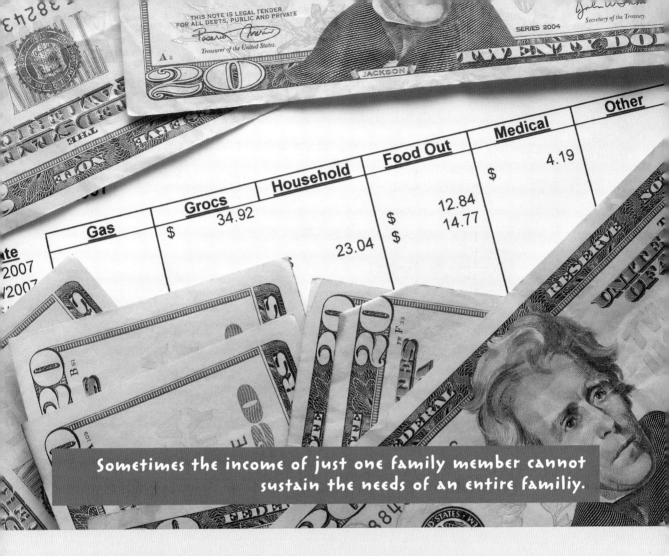

Gas	Grocs	Household	Food Out	Medical	Other
$	$ 34.92	23.04	$ 12.84 $ 14.77	$ 4.19	

Sometimes the income of just one family member cannot sustain the needs of an entire familiy.

If Mom and her sister each earn $12,000 per year, and Dad doesn't earn anything because he can't work, and the kids are too young to get jobs, their total family income is $24,000 ($12,000 + $12,000). In this case the family would not be living in poverty, having an income surplus of $892 ($24,000 – $23,108).

If the scenario is changed a bit, Dad earns $18,000 a year, Mom is a stay-at-home mom, Aunt Z is disabled and can't work, and the kids each earn $1,500 per year doing odd jobs, the total family income would then be $21,000 ($18,000 + $1,500 + $1,500). That figure falls below the poverty threshold for this family size and indicates an income deficit of $2,108 ($23,108 – $21,000).

Table 2. Child Well-Being Inside and Outside Metropolitan Areas

Family Characteristics	Year	% Metro	(Rural) % Non-Metro
Two Married Parents	2003	68	68
Related Children in Poverty	2002	16	**20**
Rel. Children in Extreme Poverty	2002	6	**7**
Rel. Children in Low Income	2002	20	**27**
One Parent Employed Full time	2002	79	**76**
Health			
Good or Excellent Health	2002	84	**82**
10th Grade Smoking Daily	2003	8	**14**
10th Grade Binge Drinking (within last two weeks)	2993	21	**26**
10th Grade Illicit Drug Use (within last thirty days)	2003	19	**22**
Education			
Adolescents Ages 16–19 Neither in School nor Working	2003	8	**10**
High School Grads Ages 25–29 Who Completed a BA or Higher	2003	30	18
Morality Rates (listed in deaths per 100,000–not percentaqes)			
Children Ages 1–4	2000	30	**42**
Children Ages 5–14	2000	17	**24**
Adolescents Ages 15–19	2000	62	**87**

Note: Bold figures indicate where rural youth are doing worse than urban youth.
Sources: Population Reference Bureau: Rural Families Data Center; U.S. 2000 Census SF3; Department of Housing and Urban Development (HUD); National Center for Health Statistics; National Institutes of Health.

These numbers might seem meaningless in the day-to-day struggle of the poor. But when it comes to a township or county qualifying for and receiving government assistance, these statistics make all the difference in the world. Many American communities receive government aid—whether dollars, resources, or intervention programs—largely based on poverty demographics. Most nations use similar systems to identify their poor.

Poor Rural Youth and Well-Being

Because more poor people live in metropolitan areas, researchers studying low-income youth tend to focus their work on city youth, and many studies on this group have been conducted. Studies limited to the rural poor—let alone poor, rural youth—are not common, but a few do exist. One such study, conducted in 2004 by the Population Reference Bureau, found that impoverished youth living in rural America not only face challenges typically associated with poor city kids, they fare worse than urban peers in several key arenas: health; mortality; cigarette, alcohol, and drug use; secure parental employment; and education outcomes (Table 2). Isolation and lack of support services in rural settings only *exacerbate* these problems.

Child *mortality rates* are of particular concern; these rates run approximately 30 percent higher in rural regions largely due to limited medical care and the hazards of rural driving. Poor, rural youth also seem to lag behind in education. Only 18 percent of young people from impoverished rural areas earn bachelor degrees by their mid-twenties, compared with 30 percent of urban youth, but many rural teens leave their rural roots for educational opportunities in metropolitan areas. This tendency might explain the wide rural/urban *disparity* in education.

Rural Realities

One problem in accurately understanding the rural poor is that many poverty studies combine urban and rural statistics. Because of the sheer numbers of city youth, urban figures sway these results, which can be misleading. Studies of urban poverty simply don't translate to rural populations. In fact, the results of such studies

Many rural youth will not have access to the same educational opportunities as urban youth.

In the United States, poor rural families are more likely to be Mexican American, Native American, or Caucasian.

sometimes add to generalizations about the rural poor that are simply not true.

For example, while urban studies show U.S. urban-poor children are more frequently Hispanic, Latin American, African American, Asian, or biracial, U.S. rural-poor children are more likely to be Mexican American, Native American, or Caucasian. Canada's rural poor are often Aboriginal. According to the Population Reference Bureau, poverty rates for urban families with children held steady or even slightly decreased over the last ten years. If one generalized this data, it might be believed that the number of rural-poor kids went down, too. It didn't. During the same period, poverty rates for rural children *increased*.

The lack of rural-specific poverty studies has also led to many misconceptions and false assumptions regarding poverty-stricken rural youth and their families. Perhaps the most *tenacious* myth is that the rural poor choose poverty because they don't want to work. First of all, many of the rural poor in the United States are not of working age. The elderly and children—including teens—make up the largest percentage of this population.

Second, contrary to popular belief, the majority of rural-poor families do have at least one employed family member. He or she just doesn't earn enough to lift the family from poverty status, and better job opportunities are few in small communities. According to a study by Iowa State University's Rural Development Center, only about 25 percent of the rural poor have no one working in the household, and this segment is predominantly elderly. That means over 75 percent of rural families living in poverty are working poor.

Another myth is that most rural-poor people are single mothers and their children. Yes, single mothers with children are more likely to end up impoverished than two-parent families, but in terms of percentages, single-mother rural families actually trail two-adult households. The Iowa State study cited earlier reports that 38 percent of the nation's rural poor are single-mother households, and over 40 percent are two-parent families. The few studies focusing on the rural poor have shown poor, rural youth more frequently come from married, employed, nonminority households than stereotypes suggest. Traditional, blanket portrayals of rural poverty simply don't hold up against reality.

America's poor, rural youth are as diverse as they are misunderstood. They are people of all races, religions, and family structures. Their families are more often employed than not, but rarely farmers. Their backyard views range from barren wilderness to forests, desert sands to shores, and mountains to grasslands. These teens deal with issues common to youth everywhere, but their struggles may be more difficult because their communities lack many services and support systems our urban centers routinely offer.

Youth gangs and violent crime are just as likely to occur in rural settings as in urban ones.

Mom? She's always stressed out. She doesn't make enough for us to live like everybody else, but she makes too much for welfare. It seems like the harder she tries, the worse it gets. That's what really hurts. I never ask her for new clothes or anything. I'd feel too guilty. So I sell drugs instead—to get my own money.—Hope, a rural West Virginia teen

Rural Poverty and Crime

Traditionally a plague of urban living, drugs, and violence are quickly spreading into small-town America. While most experts agree incidents of violent crime and drug use are lower in number in rural areas than cities (the result of less people), they are quick to point out that incident rates by percentage have closed the gap between rural and urban areas. A rural community, even a poor one, is now generally no more or less likely to encounter such problems than an urban area. The statistical probability is about the same.

Youth gangs have begun to appear in many small-town schools. More rural adolescents carry weapons to class than do urban teens. A few rural-crime rates have even surpassed those of metropolitan areas. For example, alcoholism and methamphetamine-related crime rates now exceed those of America's urban centers. Not all poor, rural youth face the same problems. For some, alcoholism and abuse are huge challenges; for others, drug addiction and meth labs are the issues; and for still others, violent crime or hate groups threaten their way of life. Lucky ones escape these problems.

But every study this author encountered does support one sweeping generalization: poverty in-and-of-itself has little to do with causing rural-youth crime. The data overwhelmingly suggests being poor by itself is not a causal factor in juvenile delinquency. Report after report confirmed the main cause by far of youth offenses (rural or urban) is parental dysfunction in either of two forms: child neglect or abuse.

"The number one risk factor for girls or boys entering our system," explains William D. Ford, Chief Juvenile Probation Officer (ret.) of Bucks County, Pennsylvania, "is abuse or abandonment by the parents. Girls who commit crimes—and there are more of them today—almost without exception were verbally, physically, or sexually abused."

Yes, poverty can complicate and even encourage juvenile crime and/or criminal tendencies, and poverty can be a symptom of other issues. But poverty alone is rarely an isolated cause of rural-youth crime.

CHAPTER 2
Dealing Desperation: Drugs and Poverty and Rural Youth

Yeah, *kids here have problems. They don't have any money, and this place is too far away from everything. There's nothin' to do but smoke weed. And nobody's parents care if you do—that's a joke—they do it, too.*

The reason we sell drugs and guns is because we can't get jobs anywhere else. Look around this place. Where would I get a job? It's hard to make any money legally here, but I don't sell drugs because I don't like to count money. My friend deals the drugs; I handle the weapons.

Dreams? [Laugh] I don't have many dreams. But I'd do just about anything for money. [Pause] I guess I really need to get out of here. — Marcus, a rural teen gang member, age sixteen, Wyoming

When you hear Marcus describe his lifestyle, it's easy to assume he comes from an inner-city neighborhood, but he doesn't. Marcus lives in a desolate, rural community in Wyoming, far from the alleys and graffiti of urban living. A flat, dry landscape makes up his turf, and dusty beer bottles litter its dirt roads. Nonetheless, Marcus has "homeys"; he's part of the North Bloods, a rural gang.

Don't be surprised. Gangs are prevalent in many rural areas, particularly in central California and on Native American and Inuit reservations. In the Navajo Nation alone, tribal police reported more than seventy-five active gangs at the recent turn of the century.

Gang activity, drug manufacturing, dealing, and addiction—and the crimes that inevitably surround each of them—have become as much a rural phenomenon in recent years as an urban one. According to FBI data, over the eight years spanning 1995 through 2002, drug-related arrests rose 21 percent in rural counties across the United States while urban rates dropped by more than 23 percent. According to a recent survey conducted by the Substance Abuse and Mental Health Services Administration, the highest rate of drug use for U.S. kids between the ages of twelve and seventeen is now in rural counties. (The latest scourge is methamphetamine.) Such statistics sound incredible or even exaggerated, but they're not.

Wyoming Woes

Courts in Lovell, Wyoming, convicted seventy people (out of a total population of just over 2,200) of drug crimes over the last two years. In 2004, methamphetamine-related crimes alone consumed over half the time and resources of the area's seven-officer police force. This drug is infecting the region like a contagious disease, and officials believe meth-related crimes will double by the end of 2005. Methamphetamines took this community completely by surprise. A recent *New York Times* article quotes Wyoming Attorney General Pat

DRUG-FREE SCHOOL ZONE

HIGH PROFILE ENFORCEMENT AREA

VIOLATIONS IN THIS AREA WILL BE AGGRESSIVELY PROSECUTED IN ACCORDANCE WITH

Drugs in schools are as much a problem in rural areas as they are in urban ones.

Law enforcement officials must face facts: Drugs can pervade any community.

Crank, "We lie to ourselves. We say Wyoming is God's country. . . . We can't have meth here." Welcome to reality.

Wyoming is the least populous state in the United States, with fewer than 500,000 residents spread over more than 100,000 square miles (258,999 square kilometers)—the federal government still classifies the entire state as frontier land—yet it has one of the most challenging methamphetamine problems in the country. Exactly how bad is the problem? One 2001 U.S. Department of Justice bulletin reported more than 40 percent of Wyoming teens in grades ten through twelve met official criteria for classification as "users," while 10 percent were addicted or drug dependent, and Wyoming's eighth-graders in general used methamphetamine at higher rates than all high school seniors nationwide. Overall, more than one in every hundred Wyoming residents (almost 6,000 people) needed substance-abuse treatment in 2001 for methamphetamine use. It's a chemical plague.

Rural Wyoming is not alone. Many Appalachian backcountry communities, once infamous for moonshine, now host crystal-methamphetamine labs. According to a 2004 *Miami Herald* article, Drug Enforcement Agency officers uncovered over 500 such labs in rural Tennessee and another 440 in Alabama in just one year. Lab explosions—a common risk in "hot" making the drug—started dozens of California and Canadian wildfires in recent years. Clearly, rural America offers several things methamphetamine suppliers find attractive: isolation, resources, and poverty's desperation.

Methamphetamine

What exactly is methamphetamine? Sometimes it's called "crank," "chalk," "speed," "crystal," "ice," "Shabu," "glass," "crystal meth," or just plain "meth." Methamphetamine is an amphetamine: a potent stimulant that temporarily increases alertness, relieves fatigue, and produces feelings of exhilaration and strength. Meth produces these pleasurable feelings by temporarily increasing the level of a *neurotransmitter*, called dopamine, in the brain.

When appropriately balanced, dopamine is a good thing; it stimulates the brain's pleasure and reward sensors. Too much, though, means trouble. There's an initial physical rush: a user's heart pounds, and he or she sweats. Once that rush subsides, the drug leaves the user extremely energetic for a time. The length of time varies with the form of the drug and with individual users, but the feeling's intensity often leads to "runs," which last for days as users ingest the drug again and again. Users frequently have so much energy they won't sleep or eat during their extended high and look desperately for ways to burn it off. That's the attraction.

Table 3. Drug Schedule

In 1970, responding to widespread drug abuse of the time, the U.S. Congress passed the Comprehensive Drug Abuse Prevention and Control Act, which is enforced by the U.S. Drug Enforcement Agency. This act provides a system for classifying drugs into five levels—for law enforcement purposes—according to two main factors: how addicting a drug is and if the drug has current, approved medical use in the United States. It is updated every year.

Classification	Addiction Potential	Approved Medical Use	Examples
Schedule I	very high	NO	heroin, marijuana, hashish, LSD, GHB, PCP, Ecstasy, peyote, mescaline
Schedule II	very high	YES	methamphetamine, cocaine, crack, methadone, opium, morphine, codeine, oxycodone
Schedule III	moderate	YES	anabolic steroids, barbiturates, testosterone
Schedule IV	low	YES	Rohypnol, Xanax, Valium, Ambien, phenobarbital
Schedule V	very low	YES	Robitussin A-C, Pediacof, Lomotil

Source: U.S. Department of Justice.

One teen described dancing for days on end; others obsessively cleaned their dusty, wooden floors with toothbrushes; some even disassembled then reassembled old cars. This kind of energy may sound highly productive, exciting, or even desirable, but only until the drug wears off. Meth-induced runs inevitably end in a dramatic "crash" characterized by extreme lethargy and depression. Side effects of the extended euphoria can range from depression or mild

Table 4. Drug Use and Duration Differences

The Substance Abuse and Mental Health Services Administration's (SAMHSA) National Clearinghouse for Alcohol and Drug Information (NCADI) offers drug profiles on most of the nation's addictive drugs. When it comes to highs, drugs are not created equal.

Class	Drug	How Used	Duration (in hours)
narcotic	heroin	injected, sniffed, smoked	3–6
narcotic	opium	oral, smoked	3–6
cannabis	marijuana	smoked, oral	2–4
cannabis	hashish	smoked, oral	2–4
stimulants	cocaine	sniffed, smoked, injected	1–2
stimulants	methamphetamine	oral, injected	2–4
stimulants	methamphetamine	smoked, inhaled (ice, crystal)	4–14

Source: SAMHSA's National Clearinghouse for Alcohol and Drug Information.

panic to violent outbursts, from hallucinations to extreme *paranoia*. No wonder users want to get high again, but doing so can result in homicidal or suicidal thoughts and actions, not to mention a host of negative effects on the heart and brain, some of which may also cause death.

Some teens believe the intense pleasure they get from methamphetamine is worth the risk of addiction. The same is true of many adults. But methamphetamine is extremely dangerous. The U.S. government classifies methamphetamine as a Schedule II drug (see Table 3), which means it is highly addictive, both physically and psychologically. It's in the same class as crack cocaine.

Law Enforcement Initiatives

Some jurisdictions and businesses are making it more difficult to obtain certain over-the-counter ingredients to produce meth. In many areas, cold and allergy medications are now kept off the shelves (much like tobacco products), requiring a store employee to get them for the customer. The amount of these medications that can be purchased at one time is also limited in some places.

The addictive quality of methamphetamine is good news for illegal drug manufacturers. Some teens can become addicted to meth with just one use, and intense, driving addictions mean greater demand, hence greater profits. For the poor, rural, jobless adolescent looking for easy money and something to do, manufacturing and selling this drug can seem like nirvana.

First, the drug is popular. Why? For some workers in economically depressed regions—especially those who engage in hard, manual labor hour after hour, day after day, at low wages—meth initially helps them get through their days, work additional hours for overtime pay, and stay up to work two and three jobs. And since potential meth addicts can become dependent with just one use, an ever-increasing market is practically guaranteed.

The drug also offers user convenience; its various forms can be ingested orally, injected, smoked, or inhaled. Plus, methamphetamine provides a lot of high for the cost. For example, cocaine is generally more expensive than meth, and cocaine's high usually lasts only one

The addictive quality of methamphetamine makes it extremely dangerous.

The relative ease of manufacturing methamphetamine makes it an attractive option for some desperate rural teens.

or two hours. Compare that rush to the eight- to fourteen-hour high smoking or inhaling meth provides (Table 4).

Second, just about anyone can make methamphetamine at home cheaply and simply using everyday substances like matchbooks, antifreeze, lye, over-the-counter cold medications, and glassware. A lab can be up and running in no time, with recipes, instructions, and manufacturing methods available on the Internet, a drugstore and a hardware store (for ingredients and utensils), and a small amount of cash. Plus meth addiction is so potent that most users will pay almost any price for another high. Combined, these factors can translate into huge profits. For someone struggling in poverty, that's tempting.

Third, "cold" cooking techniques have made meth-manufacturing processes simpler and safer. Traditional meth recipes required heating and were dangerous because batches often exploded. Law enforcement could detect these "hot" labs because they gave off pungent odors and were difficult to move. The development of cold techniques virtually eliminated these risks. Labs became portable, odorless, and nonexplosive. It's almost easy for meth manufacturers to set up individual operations and avoid detection.

Last, rural areas offer isolation. Isolation means getting caught is less likely. In desolate areas, just one or two police officers are often responsible for vast territories. The likelihood of an officer stumbling onto one lab hidden among hundreds of acres is remote. Both the individual *"entrepreneur"* and international drug rings know this.

For these reasons and more, methamphetamine production has invaded the countryside. Whereas drugs like heroin and cocaine generally come into our cities from other countries, methamphetamine is home grown and American made, and rural America is the hub of production. Yes, some labs are "super" labs (those financed, run, and protected by professional drug traffickers), but with widespread Internet accessibility (even most public libraries have it), many labs are now one- or two-person operations set up by the rural

Did You Know?

• Rural eighth-graders are 104 percent more likely to use amphetamines, including methamphetamine, than urban eighth-graders.

• Rural eighth-graders are also 50 percent more likely to use cocaine and 34 percent more likely to smoke marijuana than their urban equals.

Source: U.S. National Center on Addiction and Substance Abuse.

poor to make quick, substantial (*albeit* illegal) money with little risk of injury or detection. Rural youth are not immune to the temptation. The lure of fast cash and faster highs offers a temporary escape from boredom, poverty, and seeming powerlessness.

Portrait of Addiction

Desmond first used meth at the beginning of his senior year in high school. His unfinished senior project (without which he wouldn't graduate) was due in three days. Although he had never used drugs before, he felt he needed some extra energy to get him through the three days of work ahead. A friend recommended speed.

Desmond knew he shouldn't take it, but this was an emergency and a short-term one at that. He had to finish his project by the deadline or not graduate, and to finish on time meant pulling a few all-nighters over the next few nights. He couldn't do it without help,

Once you are addicted, drugs take control of your life.

so he bought some meth in gelatin capsules and swallowed one with water.

Almost immediately, Desmond was full of energy. The drug kept him working for six straight hours, after which he started to crash and feel lethargic and depressed. So he repeated the dose, worked frantically for more hours, crashed again, took more meth, and so on. This cycle continued until Desmond completed his project three days later. Once the project was turned in, Desmond came home, came down, and slept for thirty-six hours straight.

With the project behind him, urgency couldn't justify taking any more speed, but Desmond remembered and liked the potency he felt on it, so he began to regularly snort meth with friends on weekends. Over time, his system grew tolerant to the drug, and he needed larger or more intense quantities to produce comparable highs. He tried pills again, then injected meth directly into his veins, and eventually started smoking it without knowing that the

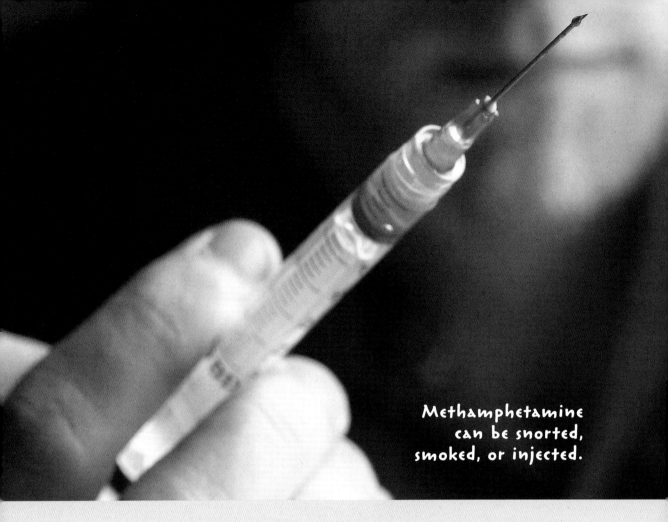

Methamphetamine can be snorted, smoked, or injected.

inhaled form of meth (called ice, crystal, ice cream, or glass) is more addictive than crack cocaine.

When his addiction reached the point of needing meth every day, Desmond turned to his parents for help. He knew he had a problem and wanted to straighten himself out before starting trade school, so his parents checked him into a government-sponsored rehab program in the nearest city, three hours away. It worked.

In this case, Desmond began his journey into addiction as a short-term aid to help him meet his commitment. It was readily available and it worked. Countless teens get started the same way: innocently. That's meth's *insidious* nature.

Other teens' naiveté, ignorance, and longing for acceptance, success, or financial freedom (or simply something to do!) open the doors to addiction. The eleven-year-old who lights her first cigarette behind the school to impress peers; the twelve-year-old who, just for entertainment, sniffs inhalants from a brown paper bag in the woods with friends; the athletic junior who takes anabolic steroids to improve his game so he can get a college athletic scholarship; older teens who get into the drug business to make easy money, especially when they've been poor their whole lives and can't find work anywhere else: the list of reasons and circumstances is as varied as it is endless.

Roots of Addiction

Desmond was lucky. He had parents who were involved in his life and willing to help him any way they could. Other students are not as fortunate. Do you remember Marcus at this chapter's opening? His story continues:

> I live with my grandma. I don't have a dad, well I do, somewhere, but I don't think he's alive. My mom, I have no idea where she is. My aunt, she's also gone. I think she went to L. A. So I live with my grandma, but she's a real pain in the a-- . . . always puttin' me down, yellin' at me. I get sick of her nagging. She just goes on and on and on . . . so I live in the shed out back. It's a piece of sh--, but at least I don't have to deal with her, and it keeps me dry when it rains.
>
> Sometimes my biological mom shows up, usually drunk. There are a lot of drunks around here. Sometimes she'll crash at my place, even stay with me for a week, but then she leaves again. I have no idea where she goes.
>
> My uncle was the first one to get me high. [Laugh] Man, he's messed up. I was only twelve.

Marcus's family life is more typical of the youth addict or drug dealer. Most young people who use drugs started because a family member or friend persuaded them to try it. That's true of both rural and urban youth. Having, in essence, no functional parent to guide him, Marcus had to figure out right from wrong for himself. Furthermore, the little family he had modeled addiction as normal behavior. For as long as Marcus can remember, alcoholism and drug abuse were the only predictable parts of day-to-day life. He didn't know any better.

Through their actions, Marcus's family unintentionally taught him powerful lessons about abandonment, irresponsibility, selfishness, and broken trust. Those are the lessons he learned best. Such lack of stability breeds remarkable feelings of insecurity in teens and sends them subconsciously scrambling for love and acceptance wherever they can find it. Rural kids are no exception.

Back in Wyoming, Marcus filled his needs with a surrogate "family"— his gang— and by selling and using drugs. Like Marcus, some poor, rural teens find financial security—often for the first time in their lives—in drug-trade-related income. But most get involved with drugs simply to ease their pain. Each high provides a moment, no matter how fleeting, in which a troubled kid can drift away from

An abusive family life can be the root of behavioral problems.

the world. Though most teens do not turn to drugs, many in a situation like Marcus's will seek connectedness or escape somehow, if not in chemical addiction, then in relationships, lifestyle choices, or other pursuits.

As discussed in the previous chapter, just being poor or rural do not cause drug addiction and drug-related crime. Even if a rural teen is destitute and desperate for money, he won't likely dismiss the *mores* a strong, stable, responsible, loving family fosters, no matter how financially needy he is, to obtain it. The main factor in almost every chronic, rural-youth drug case is not poverty. It's almost always a lack of solid, loving, family support, regardless of income.

Inhalants

Some younger rural teens abuse inhalants ("huffing," "sniffing," "inhaling") largely because they can use products found around most

Ordinary household items like these may be used as inhalants.

households, even the most rural or poorest home. Any product with toxic fumes can be inhaled (never safely) for a cheap, quick high: gasoline, markers, rubber cement, glue, cleaning fluids, paint thinner, aerosol sprays, nail polish remover, and correction fluid to name a few. If fact, inhalants are so obtainable and the process so simple that a recent survey showed 8.6 percent of all twelve-year-olds had tried huffing at least once, some starting as young as age six.

Inhaled fumes replace the oxygen all humans need with toxic gases, and no one can predict what will happen. Some inhalers indulge their huffing habit for years; others die the first time they try it. One study found that 22 percent of those who died from inhalant abuse had no history of huffing.

Interestingly, inhalant use among teens seems to decrease with age regardless of income or locality. A 2002 national, in-school survey titled "Monitoring the Future" found that while 4 percent of eighth-graders used inhalants within the previous month of the survey, only 1.5 percent of seniors had. Maturity (translation: more resistance to peer pressure) and knowledge of its dangers can account for part of the shift away from huffing, but a darker reason may also account for some of it: moving on to "real" drugs like marijuana, cocaine, meth, and so on. The same survey found by the time students reached twelfth grade, the percentage of those who used marijuana almost tripled eighth-grade levels, jumping from only 8 percent to nearly 22 percent in four years. Meth and cocaine abuse also rose with teens' ages. Heroin use remained constant.

The Impact

Under addiction's influence, otherwise responsible teenagers act in ways they would never act when sober. The *New York Times* reported that one young woman in Lovell, Wyoming, wrote bad checks in addition to running up nearly $60,000 of debt on dozens of credit cards to fund her meth habit. In a separate case, a rural Pennsylvania college student blew the entire $30,000 trust fund his mother had established for him, and to which he gained access when he turned eighteen.

Destitute teens in the clutches of addiction sometimes commit crimes. Robbery is common. Many teenage addicts break into cars, friends' homes, or other familiar places (like churches and schools) to take anything they know they can hock for cash. Then there's the

To fund their addiction, many teens turn to crime.

personal toll. One rural teen's younger brother, age thirteen, is already an addict like his big brother and his mom.

Regardless of the drug, regardless of the involvement (seller or user), drug abuse impacts real lives of real people. Addiction anywhere is bad, but when it occurs in rural, poor communities, the problem tends to be stubborn, long term, and severe. Poor, rural communities don't have the treatment options, programs, facilities, and professional help typical of cities. These communities can't afford such help, so addicted, poor, rural youth are on their own. Poverty just compounds the issue.

Clearly, not all poor kids turn to hardcore drugs and drug dealing. Neither do all rural poor kids, but two areas of addiction in which rural, poor youth are clearly worse off than their city counterparts involve alcohol and tobacco use. Both substances are legal for adult use across the United States and Canada, so one might think the chemicals in each of them aren't as harmful as other drugs. Think again.

CHAPTER 3
Deceptive Dangers: Marijuana, Alcohol, and Tobacco Use

My first cigarette? I don't know. Maybe I was ten. . . . But I do remember the first time I got drunk. [Laughs] Seventh grade. Me and two friends stole a bottle of Boones Farm from my mom's stuff and drank it until we got sick. Man, that stuff was awful. She never could afford anything good. [Shakes head] Beer's a whole lot better.

My first joint? That was ninth grade. . . . But I didn't go hard 'til this year. . . . Crystal Meth . . . Whoa, what a rush. You feel like you can do anything. . . . Sweet. Now I sell the stuff. [Grins] Had to do something to pay for my

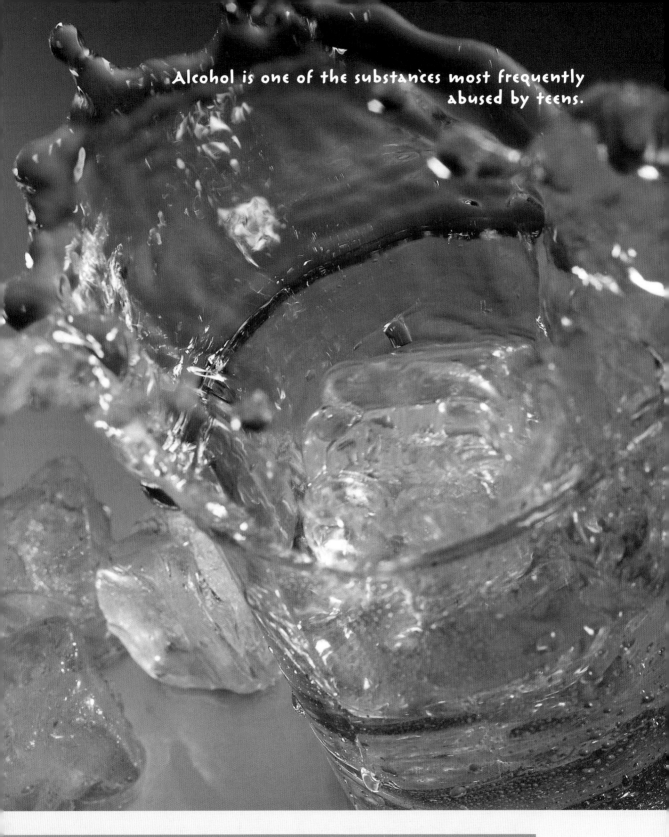

Alcohol is one of the substances most frequently abused by teens.

high, and where else was I gonna get a job? Me and my supplier, we got it all worked out.—Danny, age seventeen, north-central Pennsylvania

Cigarettes. Alcohol. Marijuana. All three have been part of Danny's rural adolescence, and scientists consider all three "gateway" drugs. What is a gateway drug? The simplest definition is a drug that leads to using other, more potent drugs. That's the hidden danger.

According to the National Center on Addiction and Substance Abuse (CASA), it's next to impossible to find a teenager who uses marijuana who didn't start with cigarettes and beer, and almost all heroin addicts used marijuana before they ever shot up. Still, you might be thinking, *my dad's been smoking and drinking for years, and he's never used drugs*. He's not alone. Most people who use nicotine, alcohol, and marijuana do so strictly recreationally and never proceed to heroin, cocaine, or meth. But those who do hard drugs almost always started there. A statistical link unquestionably exists between these three gateway drugs and the move to stronger substances.

Smoking, drinking, and marijuana use are the three most common substance-abuse issues among poor, rural teens. In 2004, the U.S. government's Office of Applied Studies found the lower a child's family income, the more likely he or she would use cigarettes. (Don't misinterpret this fact: low income and smoking is a statistical pattern, not a cause and effect.) And smoking is usually the first step.

Furthermore, the younger that kids experiment with cigarettes, drugs, and alcohol, the more likely they are to continue using them into their adult lives. CASA recently reported that among young men and women who tried smoking in elementary- and middle-school years, almost 86 percent were still smoking after they graduated from high school. Alcohol and marijuana use had similar results. Of those who had ever been drunk or high when they were younger, 83.3 percent were still getting drunk in twelfth grade, and 76.4 percent were still using.

On the other hand, CASA also reports that the person who reaches his or her twenty-first birthday without ever smoking, drinking, or getting high is virtually certain never to do so. That's the good news. So it's vital all kids understand what they're getting into and where it starts, but particularly impoverished rural youth, as they are at greater risk for substance abuse than city kids. The promise of easy money in drug dealing can be nearly irresistible to some poor.

Marijuana ("Weed," "Ganja," "Bud," "Reefer," "Pot," "Grass," "MJ," "Mari J")

For many of the same reasons meth labs have recently infiltrated rural America, marijuana plantations have dotted our countryside for many years. Rural woods and fields offer isolation and camouflage perfectly suited to growing the leafy cannabis plant and, much like tobacco, to drying its leaves. Growers only need a few seeds, a green thumb, and the right climate to get started. Like meth labs, initial cash output is minimal and the potential payoff, huge. Rural growers also run little risk of discovery.

Even rural, God-fearing Mennonite farmers and cabinetmakers have fallen prey to the marijuana trade's temptations. "Friends have urged me to hide small amounts of marijuana inside my cheeses," recounts one young Mennonite in a *Dallas Morning News* article. "Of course I said no. But everything is so expensive, and I'm having a hard time selling my goods. Plus we haven't had much rain, so the crops aren't doing well this year." Glancing down, he shakes his head. "It's getting harder to turn down such an easy $1,000."

Canadian drug enforcement agents say Mennonite drug rings account for as much as 20 percent of the marijuana smuggled into the

Freaky Farmer

In one infamous marijuana bust, neighbors of Canadian Mennonite Isaak Enns began noticing strange crops growing all over his cornfields. The concerned friends sought answers from local agricultural authorities and found that Enns was growing marijuana among his cornstalks. Unbelievably, farmer Enns was a major supplier for an international drug ring.

country each year. That makes them one of Canada's main suppliers, easily passing through customs because they look so harmless. Dozens of drug seizures have involved these gentle farmers, but most of the arrests represent one notorious Canadian-Mexican Mennonite sect that smuggles millions of dollars' worth of marijuana between Mexico and Canada inside handcrafted furniture and cheese. Hard times and the rural quality of Mennonite farms make these communities ideal havens for drug manufacturing and distribution, a fact not lost on urban drug rings.

In the late 1990s, one eastern Pennsylvania village known for its rolling farms and horse-drawn buggies was shocked when police arrested two of their young Amish men and charged them with buying and selling drugs. The early-twenty-somethings allegedly bought drugs from members of a Philadelphia gang—the Pagans—and sold them to local youth at Amish hoedowns. The two young men had been acting as cogs for the drug ring for over five years, since they were just teens.

Marijuana is a gateway drug to other more dangerous substances.

"These kids aren't used to sleeping with the devil," pointed out the district magistrate at the time. "They're used to Sunday afternoon baseball, the hoedowns, and (at worst) maybe some beer drinking."

Granted, Amish teens teaming up with Pagans is an extreme example, but drastically different cultures colliding in the drug world is becoming more common. Opposites do attract, because they each have something their complement wants or needs. The ever-increasing marriage of seemingly incompatible worlds can be seen in woods and fields across the continent. Just look for the spiky green leaves.

When I was young, I discovered it was easy to gain attention by shocking people. When I was nine years old, I smoked pot with teens. In the sixth grade a teacher found rolling papers and a tiny amount of pot in my wallet. What do you do with an eleven-year-old who has marijuana?—Chad, age eighteen, as told to Debbie Lawson in *Real Teens, Real Stories, Real Life* by T. Suzanne Eller

Based on a survey by SAMHSA, more than half of rural youths who had used marijuana in the past year obtained it for free from someone older or shared a friend's marijuana. About 10 percent of those teens got it from a relative or family member. But what if you don't have family connections? Where do rural youths buy pot? According to the SAMHSA survey—in school. The survey revealed rural youths were far more likely to purchase marijuana in middle- and high-school hallways than were urban users who tend to buy drugs off the street.

Because it's easy to grow, readily available, and relatively inexpensive compared to other drugs, marijuana continues to be the illegal drug of choice among American teens. A recent, national, drug-use survey published by the U.S. Office of National Drug Control Policy found cannabis is by far the most popular illegal substance; nearly 20 percent of all adolescents—rural and urban—from ages twelve through seventeen have used marijuana or hashish. Compare that figure to the 1.4 percent who have used methamphetamine, and you get the idea. Smoking cigarettes is even more common.

Nicotine

I can't stand waiting for the bus in the morning. There are always kids there smoking, and then by the time I get to school, I smell like a lit cigarette. All the kids stand around, cigarettes in hand, and I feel stupid 'cuz I'm the only one not smoking. It's like "Cigarettes: the breakfast of champions," and I'm the only one not in on the secret. I mean, I feel like if I'm gonna reek any-way, I may as well fit in.—Rene, a Manitoba tenth-grader

Tobacco is one of the most commonly abused substances in rural America and is just as popular with rural, poor youth. Nearly twice as many rural teens smoke as city teens. In 2001, *The Journal of Drug and Alcohol Abuse* published an article that examined what determined tobacco use specifically in rural youth. The study included nearly 1,000 ninth-grade participants from nine high schools spanning four West Virginia counties. All but one of the schools served communities with fewer than 3,000 residents, and participants were nearly equally divided between male (49.2 percent) and female (48.8 percent) respondents. The results of the study surprised even the researchers.

Nearly 32 percent of rural West Virginia ninth-graders were current smokers. That's more than twice the national average for rural youth nationwide (14 percent) and surpasses urban teens (8 percent) by nearly 400 percent. Researches defined "current smokers" as those who actively smoke from occasionally to daily.

Risk factors varied in terms of importance to these ninth-graders, but three factors consistently stood out: having friends or siblings (not parents) who smoked, not getting along with family members, and having favorable attitudes toward tobacco. All three factors were significant predictors of tobacco use. Notice that poverty is not among them.

Again, poverty alone is almost never a cause for substance abuse. That includes nicotine. Like all drug addictions, the two strongest predictors for smoking across the continent are family interactions and peer use. But unlike addictions like alcoholism, parent use (or lack of use) of tobacco products was not a significant risk factor for the West Virginia group.

Another risk factor for smoking among rural youth is a favorable overall attitude toward tobacco. By attitude, experts do not mean knowledge (or lack thereof) of tobacco's health effects. In fact, most

Alcohol and Tobacco Abuse by Metro (Urban) vs. Non-Metro (Rural) Youth

Grade	Activity	Year	(Percentage of youth participating)	
			Urban Youth	Rural Youth
10th	Smoking Daily	2003	8	14
10th	Binge Drinking (within last two weeks)	2003	21	26

Source: Population Reference Bureau's Rural Families Data Center and the National Institutes of Health's National Center for Health Statistics.

of the subjects in the West Virginia sample scored high on knowledge of nicotine use and were well aware of health hazards associated with their habit. Obviously, favorable attitude means something else.

By favorable attitude, researchers mean the general **connotations** teens have about smoking regardless of its health effects. Do they perceive smoking as cool or attractive? Does it make them feel older or more mature, even freer? Does smoking manage stress? Does it help manage weight? Do teens just like the smell of cigarettes or the feel of nicotine's high? Surprisingly, some teens still hold positive impressions of smoking, despite decades of evidence to the contrary.

Addictive Qualities of Popular Drugs

According to SAMHSA, about twelve million people are addicted to alcohol in the United States, while over four times that number, approximately fifty million, are addicted to nicotine. Nicotine is the most addictive drug of the six most popular addictive substances used in America. Their ratings are below.

Drug	Addiction	Intoxication	Withdrawal
Nicotine	6	2	4
Heroin	5	5	5
Cocaine	4	4	3
Alcohol	3	6	6
Caffeine	2	1	2
Marijuana	1	3	1

Note: The higher the number, the more serious the drug's effect.

When such attitudes are in place, they become a potent risk factor for nicotine addiction.

Regardless of what triggers which rural kids to smoke, all teens need to know that when researchers rated the six most popular drugs according to dependence (how hard they are to quit), nicotine came out on top. In other words, quitting smoking is more difficult than quitting heroin, cocaine, alcohol, caffeine, and marijuana, in that order. Nicotine is far more addictive than any of these substances.

Consider alcohol. Most people can regularly drink small amounts of alcohol, like a glass of wine with dinner, without becoming phys-

Smoking costs more than money, it also costs your health.

ically addicted to it. But according to a Partnership for a Drug-Free America tracking study, nearly 80 percent of those who smoke even sporadically develop nicotine addiction. Obviously, it's important to never start.

Poverty doesn't help the problem. Cigarettes are expensive. One might think cost alone would deter the habit, but it doesn't. That's how powerful the addiction is. In 2005, the average price of a carton of ten packs ranged from $10.00 for generic "value" cigarettes to as much as $35.00 for premium brands like Marlboro, Camel, Kool, and Newport (or $1.00–$3.50 per pack). Buying cigarettes at the local convenience store or supermarket would cost a lot more.

So, smoking is a very expensive habit. If a person smokes one pack a day, which is not uncommon, it costs between $7.00 and

$24.50 per week—minimum—to satisfy this habit. That's $28.00 to nearly $100 per month that could otherwise go toward food or clothing. For a smoker living in poverty, that choice becomes one that must be made. Yet nicotine addiction can be so irresistible that smokers would rather light up than eat or have new jeans.

Quitting costs money, too. Over-the-counter, self-help methods like nicotine patches designed to gradually decrease cravings for and dependency on nicotine cost as much as cigarettes. In 2005, one on-line retailer offered drastically reduced prices—sometimes as much as 50 percent off—on some patches, yet these products still cost from $90.00 to $240.00 for eight to twelve weeks' worth of patches.

As well intentioned as self-help methods are, addiction to nicotine—both psychological and physical—is often too powerful for smokers to break on their own. Withdrawal symptoms frequently require a doctor's oversight, and medical help is pricey. Many rural poor do not have health insurance or at least the kind that covers "wellness interventions" like addiction recovery or therapy. And unlike the urban poor, they can't just walk to a free clinic for help. Support groups are not as prevalent, or easy to get to, as they are in urban areas.

The costs of smoking or quitting aren't solely financial. We all know the health consequences of smoking: multiple cancers, chronic lung diseases, premature aging, stained teeth, and so on, and these side effects don't care where you live or how much your family makes. Clearly the best plan is to never pick up a cigarette in the first place.

Alcohol

Ya know what I like about this place? It's quiet. And it feels free. You don't have to lock your doors, you can leave your dogs outside all the time, and you can ride for miles and miles without seeing a soul.

There aren't many murders here, but a lot of people drink a lot. I mean a lot. Grown-ups. Old people. Kids from school. What else is there to do? [Laugh] Here, drinkin' is just part of life.—Ty, age fourteen, Alaska

Whether consumed in beer, wine, or liquor, alcohol is a depressant. It can lower inhibitions, reduce pain and anxiety, and produce feelings of well-being. It is more addictive than marijuana or caffeine, but not as addicting as nicotine. For the alcoholic "drying out," withdrawal symptoms are more brutal than those caused by kicking a cocaine habit cold turkey. Make no mistake: alcohol is a potent, addictive drug, and it's perfectly legal for adults.

Alcohol is a **bane** across rural America, but especially within impoverished American Indian, Alaska Native, and other Aboriginal communities. Even though SAMHSA studies have found Native parents are just as likely as other parents to talk about the dangers of substance abuse, the same studies found youths living in these communities were more likely than other American children to perceive little or no risk in drinking, and to believe that all or most students in their school get drunk at least once a week. What's even more astounding is that they also perceive less parental disapproval of underage drinking than their peers in urban America. Listen to Vanessa.

> *People around here drink to escape their problems, and they start to drink at such a young age! Kids see so much, maybe too much. . . . They see their parents and grandparents drinking, then they think it's okay for them, too. Actually most of the children on the reservation have parents who abuse alcohol. Most of the kids at school do, too. So they drink. There's nothing else to do.*—Vanessa, age fourteen, New Mexico

Boredom is a major problem for teens living in rural areas of the United States and Canada. Drinking is just one way of killing time. Sadly, it's also one way of killing other things: relationships, hopes, dreams, even life itself. Alcohol-related, fatal automobile accidents are three times more prevalent in rural reservation populations than throughout America's general population. According to the National Center for Health Statistics, the death rate for U.S. rural teens between the ages of fifteen and nineteen is more than 30 percent higher than for urban youth in the same age group. The difference is largely due to automobile fatalities. Rural roads can be deadly because of the speed wide-open roads encourage. Young drunk drivers make them even deadlier.

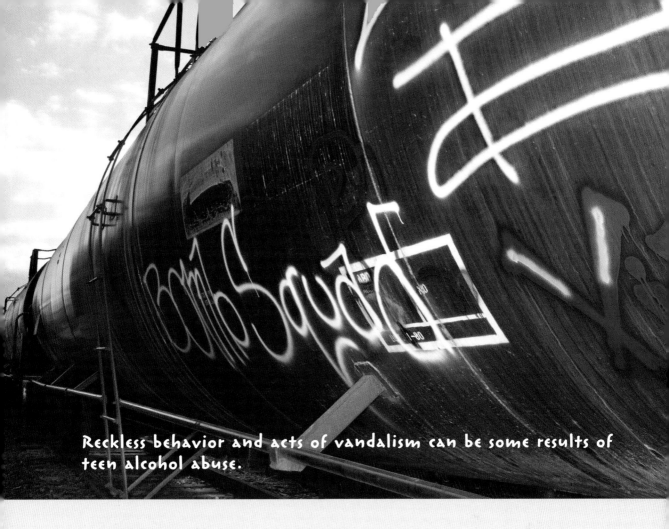

Reckless behavior and acts of vandalism can be some results of teen alcohol abuse.

Indian Health Services (IHS) and tribal hospitals also see 160 percent more cases of "first-listed" diagnoses of alcoholism and 140 percent more alcohol-related suicides than general short-stay hospitals across the continent. Rural Appalachian regions, border towns along the Rio Grande, and many of Canada's Aboriginal settlements see similar trends. Alcohol is killing the rural poor.

Because alcohol is a depressant, it often lessens inhibitions. As a result, teens who would otherwise behave responsibly can do really irresponsible things when they're drunk. Acts of vandalism and other nonviolent crimes are among the most common.

CHAPTER 4

Doomed Daring: Rural Poverty and Nonviolent Crime

There's *nothin' after school here, except if we have a game or somethin'. And even if there was, nobody ever has any money to do anything. We just hang out. That's why kids get into trouble. They're bored. There's nothin' exciting to do, so we make a little excitement of our own.*—Ronnie, a rural youth from Nova Scotia

Overturned outhouses? It happens. Smashed mailboxes? Sure. A derailed passenger train? C'mon. Bored rural teens have been entertaining themselves with acts of vandalism as long as humans have walked the earth, but their stunts usually don't result in sending dozens to the hospital, yet that's exactly what happened in 2001 in one rural Nova Scotia town.

Stewiacke is a one-stop, farming community of 1,400 located in central Nova Scotia. Railroad tracks slice through the center of town, and a bridge near the line's switching area is a popular hangout for adolescents with nothing to do. Many local kids neither have cars to take them anywhere nor money to spend even if they did. So, many Stewiacke teenagers hang out at the bridge crossing, some attempting to derail a train by tampering with a nearby railway switch and lock. One fourteen-year-old said he'd seen kids try for hours to flip the switch by throwing rocks at it. Eventually someone succeeded.

One April 2001 afternoon, witnesses saw three youths fleeing the switching area. Moments later, a Via Rail passenger train jumped a straight stretch of track in the center of town, smashing cars and a feed storage building in its chaotic path and sending dozens of passengers to regional hospitals. The train was transporting 109 passengers and fourteen crew members from Montreal to Halifax, but the switch was in the wrong position, moved with a well-aimed stone. Police charged one youth with damaging property. They questioned and released two others. The miracles are that no one died and that it hadn't happened before then.

Boredom commonly festers among the young people of rural, poor communities. Many disadvantaged towns can't support youth centers, YMCAs, or other recreational buildings. Some regions are so remote that scouts, sports clubs, and similar organizations can't offer local chapters for lack of participants and parent volunteers. And with no mall or movie theater or McDonald's or skateboarding parks, where can kids hang out? Add to that their families' own poverty and what can they do? No cell phones. No computers. No cars. No jobs. No cash. How do these teens fill idle time?

Add to that mix the fact that most rural, poor teens come from two-parent homes in which the parents work long hours at low-

Many rural areas cannot support rural youth centers, leaving teens with few outlets for healthy activities.

paying jobs. There's no one at home supervising teens between the time school ends and parents get home from work. Bored adolescents (with no money) plus nothing to do plus no supervision is a recipe destined for vandalism—or worse.

Frustration

A crime spree in rural Ramona, California, can help explain the costs of boredom. According to a *Los Angeles Times* news article, regional police arrested twenty-six local youths between the ages of eleven and seventeen for a three-month crime spree that cost the community more than $50,000. Some youths broke into the Lutheran Church on three different occasions, taking flags, robes, and even a Sunday-school teacher's desktop brass bell as souvenirs of their mischief. Others broke into the junior high school and

Mailbox Mania

According to one article in the <u>Paynesville Press</u>, a Minnesota newspaper, any week somewhere across America, a car full of rural teens is cruising local country roads looking for mailboxes to senselessly shatter. These drive-by vandals smash the boxes with everything from baseball bats to axes. How do they do it? One person drives the vehicle while at least one other teen hangs out the passenger window, taking his or her best swing at the target as the car moves by it. Most of these kids do their destructive work under night's cover during milder months.

emptied a fire extinguisher into some computers, costing the already struggling school $5,000. Two kids broke into the liquor store and stole a six-pack of beer.

Twelve teenagers, frustrated that there was neither an active skateboard club at the school nor anyplace else to skateboard, kicked off the crime spree by breaking into a school maintenance closet during a basketball game, stealing several gallons of paint, and painting skateboarding slogans all over the school's tennis courts. In separate acts, the high school also lost windows and vending machines to vandals, but the worst destruction took place at a private home. One group of teens got into an unoccupied house and used it for a party that lasted three days and caused $15,000 in destruction to the home's interior. Drunken kids (the alcohol was stolen) bashed walls, shattered mirrors, tore cabinet doors off their hinges, and ripped light fixtures out of the drywall, all in the name of entertainment.

One sixteen-year-old, who admitted letting friends into the empty house claimed, "We're not looking for trouble. It just sort of happens." A teenager who admitted his part in the school vandalism explained, "We just kind of did it. We didn't do it for any reason really, but just for the h--- of it. We were bored and broke."

Many of the parents claimed these were "good" kids, and that frustration over nothing to do led to mischief that simply "got out of hand." Some of the arrested teens told officials they succumbed to peer pressure, a *mob mentality*. Others said they did it to get even with inflexible school officials and the old-fashioned community that ignored them. Those who stole beer said they did so because they were too young to buy it and didn't have the money anyway. Whatever the causes, many of the parents eventually blamed themselves. Some claimed they were too busy to spend more time with their children:

> My wife already works two jobs, and I work all day at my job just to get home and have an acre of land to clear and cows to feed. I'm wiped out. We couldn't possibly volunteer with these kids if we wanted to.

Poverty, Drugs, and Vandalism

Clearly, poverty—both the community's and the individual's—impacts youth vandalism in rural communities. Working long hours, sometimes at multiple jobs, keeps many parents away from home. Adolescents come home to empty houses devoid of many electronic luxuries even most urban poor manage to obtain. Many poorer towns and villages offer virtually nothing for kids to do, and few teens have vehicles to travel elsewhere for entertainment. So many rural, poor kids create their own.

What happens when drugs, alcohol, or addictions enter the picture? For some teens, getting drunk or high leads to doing stupid, relatively benign stunts like driving blind through mature cornfields, spray-painting the local water tower or bridge, stealing street signs, tipping over outhouses or cows (yes, cows), even using mailboxes for drive-by batting practice. All of these pranks are real acts of vandalism that real, rural teens have pulled "for fun" while inebriated. But what about more serious offenses? Look at the record.

According to the U.S. Department of Justice's Bureau of Crime Statistics, serious property crimes and robberies have skyrocketed in impoverished rural America with the increase in rural drug activity. That's no coincidence. Penniless meth and heroin addicts, desperate to fund that next high, will do just about anything to get the necessary money. They'll target churches, schools, familiar homes—even friends' houses—and cars to steal what they can later pawn for cash to buy drugs. Some teens stoop to robbing convenience stores and gas stations to pay dealers. These kids, who already have nothing, can become desperate.

"I became quite a thief to support my habits," admits Chad, now eighteen, in *Real Teens, Real Stories, Real Life* by T. Suzanne Eller. "I stole from my parents' wallets and took anything they left lying around to hock for money. My older brother was disgusted with me. He couldn't keep anything safe from me. I even traded his shirts and shoes for cash." Chad continues, "I didn't limit my stealing to my family either. Once I stole jewelry off my neighbor's dresser."

Tragically, many poor, rural communities have also seen a rise in personal violence as alcoholism and addiction affect entire families, including teenagers. More often than not, violent youths perpetuate a cycle of abuse that began generations before them, with or without drugs. They simply don't know any other way.

Some teens react violently to drugs they've ingested. Others are so crazed, so desperate to feed their habit, they'll hurt anyone who gets

Cow-Tipping?

Poor, rural teens have looked for inexpensive ways to entertain themselves for centuries. One of the oldest acts of rural vandalism is cow-tipping. Recent rumors have labeled cow-tipping an urban legend, pure fiction, but those who spent their teens in or around cow-country know the pastime is more fact than fiction. What is it? Cow-tipping is a classic, rural prank that involves sneaking up on a standing cow in a field (at night, no less) and slamming your full bodyweight into the poor beast, tipping it over. (The fictional parts are that all cows sleep standing up and that one person can knock a full grown cow over with one shove.) Cows are inherently clumsy and have a bad sense of balance, so many of these animals actually fall over if startled and pushed with enough force. Because some cows suffer injuries when they fall (at great cost to ranchers and dairy farmers), cow-tipping is now a felony in most states.

in their way. A few youths are angry—angry at parents, circumstances, specific people, or the hand life has dealt them. Yeah, they got a raw deal, and under the restraint-lessening influence of a preferred substance, that rage can erupt. But perhaps the most tragic cases of personal violence involve rural teens who turn to violence against others out of sheer boredom or the ignorance and frustrations extreme poverty can breed.

CHAPTER 5
Deadly Dysfunction: Rural Poverty and Violence

Friday nights are the worst around here. It seems like everybody drinks, then the fighting starts. You hear all that yellin' and screamin' and bangin'—usually when you're trying to go to sleep. It's really awkward . . . you know, listening . . . and scary. Sometimes the fighting gets so bad I have to go somewhere else to spend the night.—Willow, a thirteen-year-old living on a tribal reservation

Chicago psychiatrist Carl Bell once said, "Violence is the weapon of the powerless," and two segments of America's population that perhaps feel the most powerless are the poor and the young. Combine the

A cycle of violence begins when children experience abuse at home.

two, and the likelihood of violence increases. Then add, for some, the influence of substance abuse, and it's no wonder rural America is seeing violent crime in similar percentages (not numbers) to that of American cities.

Whether urban or rural, poor communities frequently have higher rates of violence than other regions, so many experts include poverty as one risk factor for physical aggression. That can be misleading. While it is true poverty and violence often go hand in hand, it is not because one *causes* the other. When you see both issues in a teen's life, they're usually symptoms of bigger family problems.

Violence Begins at Home

According to the American Psychological Association, the single greatest predictor of violence during the teenage years is *unequivocally* a personal history of violence and/or neglect at home. The United States Department of Justice reports that approximately 70 percent of all youths arrested for violent crimes have a history of abuse or neglect at the hands of their primary caregivers. One major study conducted by the School of Criminal Justice at State University of New York found when children have a history of both abuse and neglect, they're twice as likely to become violent during teen years as adolescents from nonviolent families. This major, six-year study found that that likelihood applied equally to all socioeconomic classes; in this study, poverty wasn't found to be a significant factor.

Of course not all maltreated poor kids grow up to be violent, and not all violent adults were abused kids. Teens vary in their responses to abuse. One of the most stubborn questions in research today is why one child becomes violent when, under identical abusive conditions, another child does not. Some respond with passive acceptance, especially if they don't know any other way to live. Others try to fight back. Most struggle with self-blame (mistakenly), and virtually all victims of familial abuse experience a complicated range of emotions, including anger, that's likely to erupt on someone, sometime, someway. Tragically, violent behavior, like poverty, tends to plague generations.

One twelve-year-old from Minnesota admits, "I use violence 'cause sometimes I get so frustrated with people that it's easier to smack 'em than to talk with them." He quickly adds, "That's what Dad does." A California teen explains, "I learned from my father that punching and slapping are what you do when someone makes you angry. When I get mad, I'm going to hit someone, anyone, whoever is in my way." Whether rich or poor, violent and neglectful parents often create violent kids, but poverty can and does make things worse.

The trials of poverty can push a stressed-out teen over the edge.

Poverty and Violence

Many impoverished children grow up in homes where financial pressures overburden parents. Routine childhood behaviors about which middle-class parents rarely give a second thought can eat away at struggling caregivers: leaving a light on (if they even have electricity), asking for favorite foods, or needing a coat or lunch money yet again. Poverty for these families means daily reminders of what they don't have, often accompanied by a continually building frustration.

If a parent or teen is already prone to violence, poverty's stressors can fuel and ignite its outburst. Stress acts much like heated air in a

Ask her about basketball and Joy will tickle your ears all afternoon, but she won't talk about her family. If any question hits too close to home, she adeptly changes the subject. When Joy finally does open up, she sheepishly describes her living conditions: a dilapidated, wooden structure (barely a house) deep in Appalachian country, with neither heat nor running water. The shack doesn't even have a front door. "Winters are hard," she admits.

Joy's mom spends most of her time in a wheelchair after suffering four strokes—she's only forty-two—and her dad is an alcoholic. Intense fighting and physical abuse are common in Joy's house, particularly when her dad is drunk, which is more often than not. (Injuries from repeated beatings possibly caused her mother's strokes.) At times home life is so unbearable that Joy finds other places to stay.

pressure cooker or lava in a volcano, building until it finally explodes. Sometimes the eruption's target is a neighbor or acquaintance (as in the example that opened this chapter). Tragically, it's usually another family member: a spouse, child, or pet. If violent abusers also use alcohol or drugs, these substances remove or at least compromise what few inhibitions keep them in check.

Remember, poverty alone rarely triggers violence, but if a parent or teen already lacks a healthy family history and the moral compass one usually *imparts*, a seemingly insignificant trigger can push that person over the edge. Maybe it's hate or jealousy, or some twisted

High School Problems Over the Years

1950

Talking out of turn

Chewing gum

Whistling/catcalls/noise

Running in the hall

Cutting in line

Dress code violations

Littering

2000

Drug abuse

Alcohol abuse

Rape

Suicide

Assault

Pregnancy

Robbery

sense of entitlement. Perhaps someone hurt them, and they want to get even. Maybe they're just looking for someone to blame for their misery. Whatever the final straw, some rural poor cross the line into violence, occasionally with fatal results.

Seventeen-year-old convicted murderer Laurie Tackett talks about one of her accomplices, Melinda Loveless, sixteen: "I didn't think she was going to go that far [murder]. It wasn't . . . 'I can't believe I'm doing this,' it was . . . 'I can't believe this is happening.' I told her it was stupid. . . . Shanda hugged me. She begged me not to let Melinda do it. She was crying . . . there wasn't anything I could do."

All four of the girls involved in twelve-year-old Shanda Sharer's torture and murder have never denied what they did. Instead, they've tried to rationalize their actions or blame each other. Why

The behavior a child learns at home will influence him his entire life.

High school teachers used to have to worry about petty problems like passing notes and chewing gum. Now drug abuse and violence are major concerns.

did these rural Indiana girls brutally kill one of their own on a dirt road fifteen miles (24.1 kilometers) out of town? Shanda was pretty, popular, and better off economically than they were, and they perceived her as a threat to one of their relationships.

Petty jealousy: that was it. The brutality of this crime clearly indicates some history of maltreatment at home, but simple jealousy is what pushed these kids over the edge. Their rural locality enabled them to torture Shanda for hours without anyone hearing her screams, and their poverty dictated the weapons: hands, fists, feet, knees, a paring knife, a piece of old rope, a tire iron, Windex, gasoline, and matches—whatever was easily accessible.

Violence at School

It's a fact: teenagers pick on other teenagers. The FBI's National Incident-Based Reporting System and the Office of Juvenile Justice and Delinquency Prevention report that adolescents under eighteen target other under-eighteen-year-olds for violent crimes more than twice as often as they target any other age group. And we're not talking about a harsh gesture or shove in line any more.

Teen-on-teen assaults are eight times the number of teen-on-adult attacks. The most likely years for being either victim or victimizer are between the ages of fourteen and seventeen. The most likely time of day for teen-on-teen violence is between two and four on weekday afternoons, when school is out and parents are still at work. Kids are hurting kids like never before, and that's true in rural America, too.

One of the problems is that smaller, individual, rural schools are commonly closing for financial reasons in favor of large, mega-schools. Rural poor teenagers coming from more *homogenous* schools (where almost everybody's poor) suddenly find themselves thrown in among middle-class teens from all over their counties. That can feel threatening, degrading, or at least awkward.

> *Many poor kids around here are brought up feelin' self-con-scious about bein' from eastern Kentucky. I could barely talk to people or look them in the eye. . . . Y'all have to understand that bein' poor and from the South, you just grow up without any confidence. . . . I knew all the stereotypes people had about me. "Hillbilly. Redneck. White trash." That used to really hurt.*—
> Jacob, age eighteen, Kentucky

Some poor kids get singled out and bullied because of where they live or the clothes they wear. Frustration and the hurt of rejection build. Increased exposure to violence in the movies, on TV, in gaming, and on the Internet doesn't help. These kids start screaming inside, and the only way many of them know to release it is by what they've seen at home or elsewhere. That includes using guns.

Murder in Rural America

Jonesboro, Arkansas. Springfield, Oregon. Pearl, Mississippi. Edinboro, Pennsylvania. All exemplify small-town America, and all are homes to mass-murdering teens. Over time, other teens mercilessly bullied each of these killers, and their anger first simmered then raged. As rare as such killings are, could these crimes have happened in urban schools? Probably not. The culprits would have never made it through the doors.

According to the American Psychological Association, many psychologists believe the recent wave of school shootings in rural America reflects complacency among rural school officials (compared to their city equals). Most urban schools recognize the problem of increased gun violence among teens and have installed weapon-control measures like metal detectors, security systems, and

The change from small-town schools to regional high schools has increased problems. Some poor kids get singled out and teased because of their clothes or background.

security personnel. Others have beefed up antiviolence programs and local policing. Rural schools generally aren't as savvy, or the money to pay for such measures is lacking.

"I had one principal tell me there's no violence in his school," asserts a school psychologist who evaluates juvenile offenders for the court system. "I just rolled my eyes. It's there. He just doesn't see it."

Rural youths, even poor ones, have greater access to guns. Many rural families use guns to control damaging animal populations like birds, groundhogs, rabbits, deer, bear, fox, or moose. Some rural poor also hunt for food or income, so shotguns and rifles commonly hang on the walls of many rural homes. If a student has a grudge and a family history of dysfunction, an easily accessible gun may be there to settle the score.

In 1996, a rural California seventeen-year-old lured his best friend on an after-school turkey-shooting, beer-drinking adventure, something they'd often done before. The real purpose of this "adventure" was to confront him about rumors the sixteen-year-old had supposedly spread. Both had shotguns. After a brief argument, the first boy disarmed his friend, emptied five blasts into the boy's body, then picked up the second rifle and shot him in the face—all over a silly rumor.

Assault and Rape

Teen assault and rape are far more common rural occurrences than murder. According to the FBI Uniform Crime Reports, the state of Alaska reported more than double the average rate for rape in the general U.S. population. (Keep in mind that 90 percent of Alaska cannot be reached by any road system. That's about as rural as it gets!) A 2003 report issued by the National Sexual Violence Research Center in Enola, Pennsylvania, found that sexual assault is actually more prevalent outside cities and suburbs nationwide than within metropolitan areas, but it's also less likely to be reported. That's even more true if the victim is poor.

First, the victim doesn't have the money for medical attention or legal services. Second, chances are the local sheriff, judge, and doctor know the assailant(s). Third, word spreads quickly in small communities, often wrongly shaming the victim. In fact, in some remote areas, the Enola report concluded, local attitudes may even appear "relatively accepting" toward sexual assault and other relational violence. These trends are puzzling, but one theory suggests that rural poverty is indicative of lower levels of education, and less education can breed ignorant attitudes concerning forcible rape and assault.

Rural Crime and Poverty: Violence, Drugs, and Other Issues

Clearly, poverty is linked to rural crime. Whether it's merely a contributing factor that potentially shapes criminal attitudes or it actively creates the stressors that trigger criminal behavior, poverty lurks behind the scene. From manufacturing and selling drugs to personal substance abuse, from vandalism to theft and robbery (or even rape and murder), the boredom, the lack of resources, and the lack of education America's poor, rural teens face can't help but contribute to delinquency.

That said, keep in mind that this book is about poverty's influence on rural crime. The reality is very few of America's rural poor teens engage in criminal acts of any kind. The overwhelming majority are average, law-abiding teenagers who are no different than you or I.

If you find yourself needing help in any area on which we've touched in this book, you're not alone. Every day thousands face similar struggles across America. A few resources that might help you are listed under "For More Information" on page 91. Please use them.

Further Reading

Bender, David, and Bruno Leone (eds.). *Juvenile Crime: Opposing Viewpoints*. San Diego, Calif.: Greenhaven Press, Inc., 1997.

Bennett, William J. *Body Count: Moral Poverty . . . and How to Win America's War Against Crime and Drugs*. New York: Simon & Schuster, 1996.

Blue, Rose. *Working Together Against Hate Groups*. New York: The Rosen Publishing Group, 1994.

Eller, T. Suzanne. *Real Teens, Real Stories, Real Life*. Tulsa, Okla.: River Oak Publishing, 2002.

Esherick, Joan. *Prisoner Rehabilitation: Success Stories and Failures*. Philadelphia, Pa.: Mason Crest Publishers, 2006.

Goodwin, William. *Teen Violence*. San Diego, Calif.: Lucent Books Incorporated, 1998.

Guernsey, JoAnn Bren. *Youth Violence*. Minneapolis, Minn.: Lerner Publications Company, 1996.

Hong, Maria. *Family Abuse: A National Epidemic*. Springfield, N.J.: Enslow Publishers, Inc., 1997.

Hyde, Margaret O., and John F. Setaro. *Drugs 101: An Overview for Teens*. Brookfield, Conn.: Twenty-First Century Books, 2003.

Kelleher, Michael D. *When Good Kids Kill*. Westport, Conn.: Praeger Publishers, 1998.

Kronenwetter, Michael. *Prejudice in America: Causes and Cures*. New York: Franklin Watts, 1993.

Newton, David E. *Teen Violence: Out of Control*. Springfield, N.J.: Enslow Publishers, Inc., 1995.

Williams, Mary E. (ed.). *Hate Groups: Opposing Viewpoints*. San Diego, Calif.: Greenhaven Press, Inc., 2004.

For More Information

Ameristat Population Reference Bureau: www.ameristat.org

Canadian Council on Social Development: www.ccsd.ca

Canadian Rural Partnership: www.rural.gc.ca/home_e.phtml

Center on Juvenile and Criminal Justice
• Myths and Facts about Youth and Crime:
www.cjcj.org/jjic/myths_facts.php

Child Welfare League of America: www.cwla.org

Children Now: www.childrennow.org

Children's Defense Fund: www.childrensdefense.org

Childwatch International: www.childwatch.uio.no

The Crime Library: www.crimelibrary.com

Department of Health and Human Services
• Administration for Children and Families: www.acf.dhhs.gov
• Children and Youth Policy: http://aspe.os.dhhs.gov/hsp/hspyoung.htm

Department of Justice Canada: www.canada.justice.gc.ca

Federal Bureau of Investigation Uniform Crime Reporting Program:
www.fbi.gov/ucr/addpubs.htm

Kids Count: www.aecf.org/kidscount

National Center for Children in Poverty: www.nccp.org

National Clearinghouse on Child Abuse and Neglect Information:
http://nccanch.acf.hhs.gov

National Crime Prevention Council:
www.ncpc.org/ncpc/ncpc/?pg=2088-11108

National Sexual Violence Resource Center
• Sexual Assault in Rural America: www.nsvrc.org/rural_booklet.pdf

Rural Assistance Center: www.raconline.org/info_guides

Rural Poverty Research Center: www.rprconline.org

Rural School and Community Trust: www.ruraledu.org

Rural Womyn Zone: www.ruralwomyn.net

Save the Children: www.savethechildren.org

Statistics Canada (Government of Canada): www.statcan.ca

Substance Abuse and Mental Health Services Administration (SAMHSA): http://oas.samhsa.gov

U.S. Census Bureau
- Poverty Statistics: www.census.gov/hhes/www/poverty.html
- State and County Quick Facts: http://quickfacts.census.gov

U.S. Department of Health and Human Services: aspe.hhs.gov

U.S. Department of Justice
- Office of Juvenile Justice and Delinquency Prevention: www.ncjrs.org/html/ojjdp
- Office of Justice Programs: www.ojp.usdoj.gov
- Bureau of Justice Assistance: www.ojp.usdoj.gov/BJA

What Kids Can Do, Inc: www.whatkidscando.org

Publisher's note:
The Web sites listed on this page were active at the time of publication. The publisher is not responsible for Web sites that have changed their addresses or discontinued operation since the date of publication. The publisher will review and update the Web-site list upon each reprint.

Glossary

Aboriginal: A member of any of the peoples who inhabited Canada before the arrival of European settlers.

albeit: Even though.

Appalachia: The North American region covering the southern Appalachian Mountains, and extending through southwestern Pennsylvania through West Virginia and parts of Kentucky and Tennessee to northwestern Georgia.

bane: Something that continually causes problems or misery.

connotations: Additional meanings, implications, or senses associated with or suggested by a word or phrase.

Deep South: A cultural and geographical region of the United States; although the breakdown varies, South Carolina, Alabama, Georgia, Louisiana, and Mississippi usually make up the Deep South.

demographers: People who study human populations, including their size, growth, density, and distribution, and birth, marriage, disease, and death statistics.

disparity: Difference.

entrepreneur: Someone who takes the initiative to start a business.

exacerbate: Make a bad situation worse.

homogenous: Having a uniform composition or structure.

imparts: Gives something a particular quality.

insidious: Slowly harmful or destructive.

mob mentality: A collective consciousness; groupthink.

mores: Customs and habits as they reflect moral standards of a particular group.

mortality rates: The numbers of deaths in a particular place or group compared with the total number of residents in that location or members of that group.

neurotransmitter: A chemical that carries messages between different nerve cells.

paranoia: Irrational suspicions and delusions.

shantytown: A settlement consisting of crudely built shacks.

tenacious: Tough, holding fast to something.

unequivocally: Done in a manner not allowing doubt or misinterpretation.

Bibliography

American Psychological Association. http://www.apa.org.

Ameristat Population Reference Bureau. http://www.ameristat.org.

Butler, Don. "Rampage Launched a New Justice Concept." *Calgary Herald*, September 19, 2004, sec. B, p. 1.

Butterfield, Fox. "Across the Rural Midwest, Drug Casts a Grim Shadow." *New York Times*, January 4, 2004, national edition, sec. 1.

Canada Rural Partnership. http://www.rural.gc.ca.

Canadian Council on Social Development. http://www.ccsd.ca.

Canadian Press. "Youth Charged in N.S. Train Derailment: Disbelief, Sadness in Rural Community." *Edmonton Journal*, April 15, 2001, final edition, p. A6.

Census Canada. http://www.12.statcan.ca/english/census01.

Center on Juvenile and Criminal Justice. http://www.cjcj.org/jjic/myths_facts.php.

Chesney-Lind, Meda, and Randall G. Shelden. *Girls, Delinquency and Juvenile Justice*. Belmont, Calif.: Wadsworth/Thompson Learning, 2004.

Child Trends. http://www.childtrends.org.

Child Welfare League of America. http://www.cwla.org.

Children Now. http://www.childrennow.org.

Children's Defense Fund. http://www.childrensdefense.org.

Childwatch International. http://www.childwatch.uio.no.

Clark, Sarah J., Lucy A. Savitz, and Randy K. Randolph. "Rural Children's Health." *Western Journal of Medicine*, February 1, 2001, 142.

Coolican, Patrick. "Study: Rural Kids at Disadvantage." *Seattle Times*, December 5, 2003.

The Crime Library. http://www.crimelibrary.com.

Department of Children and Family Services—Illinois. http://www.state.il.us/dcfs.

Department of Health and Family Services—Wisconsin. http://www.dhfs.state.wi.us.

Department of Health and Human Services, Administration for Children and Families. http://www.acf.dhhs.gov.

Department of Health and Human Services, Children and Youth Policy. http://aspe.os.dhhs.gov/hsp/hspyoung.htm.

Department of Justice Canada. http://www.canada.justice.gc.ca.

Dierker, Lisa C., Tynette Solomon, Peter Johnson, Susan Smith, and Alice Farrell. "Characteristics of Urban and Non-urban Youth Enrolled in a Statewide System-of-Care Initiative Serving Children and Families." *Journal of Emotional and Behavioral Disorders*, December 22, 2004, 236.

Families and Work Institute. http://www.familiesandworkinst.org.

Federal Bureau of Investigation Uniform Crime Reporting Program. http://www.fbi.gov/ucr/addpubs.htm.

Fritz, Mark. "With Drug Arrests, Urban Grit Smashes Amish Life." *Los Angeles Times*, June 25, 1998, home edition, sec. A, p. 1.

Grimm, Fred. "Maybe Rural Life Ain't What It's Cracked Up to Be." *Miami Herald*, December 26, 2004, F1 edition, sec. B, p. 5.

Henry, Patrick. "Special Report Part 5: Juvenile Justice—The War Within; One Rural Judge's Approach; Keeping Kids Close to Home." *Arkansas Democrat-Gazette*, June 28, 1998. http://www.ardemgaz.com/prev/juvenile/day5sidec.asp.

Herivel, Tara, and Paul Wright. *Prison Nation: The Warehousing of America's Poor*. New York: Routledge, 2003.

Horn, Kimberly, Xin Gao, Geri A. Dino, and Sachin Kamal-Bahl. "Determinants of Youth Tobacco Use in West Virginia." *American Journal of Drug and Alcohol Abuse*, February 1, 2000, 125.

Jacobs, Nancy R., and Jacquelyn F. Quiram, eds. *Child Abuse: Betraying a Trust— The Information Series on Current Topics*. Wylie, Tex.: Information Plus, 1999.

Jacobs, Nancy R., and Jacquelyn F. Quiram, eds. *Violent Relationships—The Information Series on Current Topics*. Wylie, Tex.: Information Plus, 1999.

Joint Center for Poverty Research. http://www.jcpr.org.

Kids Count. http://www.aecf.org/kidscount.

Library and Archives Canada. http://www.collectionscanada.ca.

Ludlow, Randy. "Bitter Lesson: Community Reflects on Consequences of Prank as Murder Trial Begins." *Columbus Dispatch*, February 29, 2004, sec. D, p. 1.

Major, Aline K, Arlen Egley Jr., James C. Howell, Barbara Mendenhall, and Troy Armstrong. "Youth Gangs in Indian Country." *OJJDP Juvenile Justice Bulletin*, March 2004.

Midwest Regional Center for Drug Free Schools and Communities. http://www.ncrel.org/sdrs/areas/issues/envrnmnt/drugfree.

National Center for Children in Poverty. http://www.nccp.org.

National Clearinghouse on Child Abuse and Neglect Information. http://nccanch.acf.hhs.gov.

National Crime Prevention Council. http://www.ncpc.org/ncpc/ncpc/?pg=2088-11108.

National Poverty Center. http://www.npc.umich.edu.

National Sexual Violence Resource Center, Sexual Assault in Rural America. http:// www.nsvrc.org/rural_booklet.pdf.

Nicotine Rx. http://www.nicotinerx.com.

North Central Region Educational Library. http://www.ncrel.org.

Ohio State University Poverty Fact Sheet Series, Rural Poverty. http://ohioline.ose.edu/hyg-fact/5000/5709.html.

Population Reference Bureau's Rural Families Data Center. http://www.prb.org/rfdcenter.

Poverty Research Center. http://www.ukcpr.org.

Public Health Institute. http://www.phi.org.

Rural Assistance Center. http://www.raconline.org/info_guides.

Rural Family Medicine. http://www.ruralfamilymedicine.org.

Rural Poverty Research Center. http://www.rprconline.org.

Rural School and Community Trust. http://www.ruraledu.org.

Rural Sociology Society. http://www.ruralsociology.org.

Rural Womyn Zone. http://www.ruralwomyn.net.

Save the Children. http://www.savethechildren.org.

Schiraldi, Vincent. "Making Sense of Juvenile Homicides in America." *ABA Criminal Justice Magazine*, 1994. http://www.abanet.org/crimjust/juvjus/13-2msj.html.

Slovak, Karen. "Gun Violence and Children." *Health and Social Work*, May 1, 2002, 104.

Sniffin, Michael J. "Nation's Crime Rate Keeps Dropping." *Associated Press*, May 17, 1998.

Statistics Canada. http://www.statcan.ca.

Stodghill, Ron, and Julie Grace. "A Train Hop to Tragedy." *Time*, July 21, 1997, 30.

Substance Abuse and Mental Health Services Administration (SAMHSA). http://oas.samhsa.gov.

U.S. Census Bureau, How the USCB Measures Poverty. http://www.census.gov/hhes/poverty/povdef.html.

U.S. Census Bureau, Income Statistics. http://www.census.gov/hhes/www/income.html.

U.S. Census Bureau, Low Income Uninsured Children by State. http://www.census.gov/hhes/hlthins.

U.S. Census Bureau, Poverty Statistics. http://www.census.gov/hhes/www/poverty.html.

U.S. Census Bureau, State and County Quick Facts. http://quickfacts.census.gov.

U.S. Department of Agriculture. http://www.nal.usda.gov.

U.S. Department of Health and Human Services, EZ/EC Communities Home Page. http://aspe.hhs.gov/ezec.

U.S. Department of Health and Human Services, Poverty Guidelines, Research, and Measurement. http://aspe.hhs.gov/poverty.

U.S. Department of Health and Human Services. http://aspe.hhs.gov.

U.S. Department of Justice, Bureau of Justice Assistance. http://www.ojp.usdoj.gov/BJA.

U.S. Department of Justice, Drug Enforcement Administration Diversion Control. http://www.deadiversion.usdoj.gov.

U.S. Department of Justice, Office of Justice Programs. http://www.ojp.usdoj.gov.

U.S. Department of Justice, Office of Juvenile Justice and Delinquency Prevention. http://www.ncjrs.org/html/ojjdp.

What Kids Can Do. http://www.whatkidscando.org.

World Hunger Year. http://www.worldhungeryear.org.

Zachariah, Holly. "Five Face Vandalism Charges in Shootings at Amish Farms." *Columbus Dispatch*, November 15, 2000, p. B6.

Zolper, Thomas. "N.J. Crime Down Nine Percent." *Record* (Bergen County)," September 1, 1999, sec. A, p. 1.

Zremski, Jerry. "Study Tries to Gauge Risk of Violence in Schools." *Buffalo News*, August 29, 2001, final edition, p. B1.

Index

Aboriginals 11, 12, 15, 22, 62, 63
alcohol 20, 47, 49, 50, 51, 56, 60, 61, 62, 63, 68, 70, 77
alcoholism 25, 42, 56, 61, 63, 70, 77
Appalachia 11, 12, 15, 31, 63, 77, 88

Canada 11, 12, 15, 22, 47, 53, 62, 63
cigarettes 20, 41, 49, 51, 55, 57, 59, 60, 61
cocaine 33, 34, 37, 38, 40, 45, 51, 58, 62
cow-tipping 71
crime 13, 22, 24, 25, 43, 45, 63, 67, 68, 70, 74, 75, 80, 84, 85
        in schools 81, 82

drugs
        selling 34, 42, 52, 53, 85
        using 37, 42, 51

FBI 28, 81, 84

gangs 24, 25, 27, 28, 42, 53
guns 27, 82, 83, 84

inhalants 41, 42, 43, 44, 45

marijuana 38, 45, 51, 52, 53, 55, 58, 61
methamphetamine 25, 28, 30, 31, 32, 33, 37, 38, 39, 40, 45, 49, 51, 52, 55, 70
        manufacture 34, 37

murder 78, 82, 84, 85

Native Americans 22, 28, 62

poverty 6, 11, 16, 17, 19, 23, 85
        statistics 11, 12, 22, 23
        studies 20, 23, 25
        threshold 17, 18
        urban 20, 22

quitting 58, 60, 61

rape 78, 84, 85

sexual assault 84, 85
stealing 68, 70

tobacco 34, 37, 49, 52, 56

vandalism 63, 65, 67, 69, 70, 71, 85
violence 24, 71, 73, 74, 75, 76, 77, 78, 81, 82, 84
        in schools 81, 82, 83

Picture Credits

Corbis 14, 21, 26, 46, 72
DEA, www.usdoj.gov/dea 35
fotolia.com
    Dmitry Bokov 22
    godfer 74
    Jim Parkin 29
    Kimberly Reinick 18
    Sergey Zelenovskiy 10
istock.com 36, 54
    M. Eric Honeycutt 8
    John Norton 24
    Eric Simard 76
    Karen Squires 79
Jupiter Images 17, 30, 39, 40, 43, 44, 48, 50, 59, 60, 63, 64, 67, 80, 83
National Park Service, www.nps.gov 13

To the best knowledge of the publisher, all other images are in the public domain. If any image has been inadvertently uncredited, please notify Harding House Publishing Service, Vestal, New York 13850, so that rectification can be made for future printings.

Biographies

Author

Jean Otto Ford was born and raised in a rural region of northern Pennsylvania, where dusty roads, county fairs, and "nothin'-to-do-on-a-Saturday-night" shaped her youth. Most of her childhood was idyllic, but in her teens she also witnessed first-hand the dangers poverty, rural boredom, and isolation can breed. Today she is a freelance author, writer, award-winning artist, and public speaker. She resides in Perkasie, Pennsylvania, with her husband, Michael, and their teenage children Kristin and Kyle, and golden retriever Gracie. *Rural Crime and Poverty: Violence, Drugs, and Other Issues* is the eighth educational title she has written for Mason Crest.

Series Consultant

Celeste J. Carmichael is a 4-H Youth Development Program Specialist at the Cornell University Cooperative Extension Administrative Unit in Ithaca, New York. She provides leadership to statewide 4-H Youth Development efforts including communications, curriculum, and conferences. She communicates the needs and impacts of the 4-H program to staff and decision makers, distributing information about issues related to youth and development, such as trends for rural youth.